Billy the Kid
Dead or Alive?

Billy the Kid
Dead or Alive?

Two Western Short Stories

by
Ellis Ash

Cleanan Press, Inc.
Roswell, New Mexico
USA

Billy the Kid, Dead or Alive?
Two Western Short Stories

The selection from *The Authentic Life of Billy, the Kid* has been broken into shorter paragraphs to improve readability. Original spelling, grammar, and punctuation have been retained.

Thanks go to the Tuesday Writers Group for comments and suggestions, and to Robin Angel, proofreader extraordinaire.

ISBN: 978-0692300305
Print Edition 1.1 CS (11/14)
Also available as an ebook.

Published by:
Cleanan Press, Inc.
401 West Vista Parkway
Roswell, NM 88201 USA

www.cleananpressbooks.com

Table of Contents

Preface

Legend says Billy the Kid killed 21 men, one for each year of his short life.

True? Who knows?

Does it matter? Not when imagination rules.

Filmmakers have created more movies about this young outlaw than about any other person, living or dead. Hundreds of tales already fill the bookshelves with his ever-expanding saga.

Here are two more stories. I hope you enjoy them.

May Billy's legend continue to grow!

Ellis Ash
Santa Fe, New Mexico

Bastille Day

(Thank you, Larry, for the idea for this story, and for bringing me to Paris to celebrate Bastille Day.)

BRILLIANT FLASHES ripped the darkened sky!

Thunderous booms drowned out excited murmurs rippling through the expectant crowds.

The elegantly bewhiskered gentleman struggled to calm himself.

Fireworks! Just Bastille Day fireworks . . . relax . . . not cannon, not gunfire . . . just relax . . . relax.

And yet, something felt wrong, foreboding, eerie, fateful, as the acrid smell of burnt gunpowder drifted in the night air.

Were those waking nightmares coming back again? The screaming, the dying—Yanks and Rebs alike?

No . . . something different.

The one-time soldier had long since come to terms with the horrors of Shiloh. No, tonight, something else pulled at his soul. Something mysterious. Something obscure. Something that crept through his being, refusing to emerge into awareness.

A feeling, just a feeling, nothing more, nothing real . . . yet, oddly, accompanied by images of that infernal youngster's bucktoothed grin and that place so far away.

The distinguished gentleman pulled himself back to his present surroundings.

I am Lew Wallace, he reminded himself, *former Governor of New Mexico Territory, now, newly appointed Envoy Extraordinary and Minister Plenipotentiary to the Ottoman Empire. I must remember my position.*

He glanced at his wife and smiled to himself. She was relishing Paris. They were stopping here on their way to Constantinople to take up his long-desired new post. Long-desired because it brought him so close to his beloved Holy Land—and because it removed him from that hell-hole, New Mexico.

Today, all Paris was commemorating Bastille Day, a celebration of Freedom.

Ah . . . freedom.

Yes! A spectacular celebration of freedom for a nation. And a celebration of his personal freedom as well. Freedom from his painful three-year stint as Governor of that wretched place. Freedom from having to think about it or its miserable inhabitants ever again.

The new Minister Plenipotentiary hastily surveyed the rest of the diplomatic delegation. Most were enjoying the fireworks.

Red bursts illuminated upturned faces, including those of the American Ambassador and his wife, but Susan had looked away, bowing her head. Perhaps she, too, felt the strange foreboding. Or, maybe she was just tired.

The day had already been a long one. A morning military parade on the outskirts of Paris under a hot July sun, then the extended banquet at the Embassy. Exquisite food and wine. His mouth watered at the recollection—the delicate smokiness of Norwegian salmon, the full-bodied 1875 Chateau Lafite arriving with the succulent roast beef. Later, the fragrant sweetness of ripe dessert peaches topped with vanilla-scented cream—ah, heavenly.

But oh, the company! Wallace couldn't decide which was worse, making dinner conversation with that ninny of an Ambassador's wife or being forced to listen to the Ambassador himself expound his own pet theories about the Christ.

Ever since the Governor had finished writing *Ben Hur,* everyone wanted to tell him their ideas for a book, or share their own interpretations of events surrounding the Crucifixion and Resurrection.

The good Ambassador was no exception.

"If Pontius Pilate had simply turned Jesus loose, no one would have ever heard of the Nazarene," he had proclaimed to his dinner guests.

"You know, we have that cowardly governor of Judea to thank for creating the whole story of the Christ. If Pilate had had the intestinal fortitude to let Jesus go free— it was within his power as governor, you understand—that lowly carpenter would have simply slipped into oblivion, just one more false Messiah, one more wandering nobody searching for fame and followers."

The Ambassador continued, his enthusiasm increasing, "*All* the interest, *all* the stories, *all* the devotion down through the centuries came because of the action—or rather, the inaction—of that one pusillanimous governor."

"Blasphemy!" squeaked the Ambassador's wife while the others around the table stared silently, mouths agape.

"Quiet, dear!" The Ambassador turned and shot his wife a black look. Clearly, he had heard this comment before.

"Now, that may not have been Pilate's intention," he returned to his discourse. "The man was just bowing to political pressure, just trying to protect his own career, but his actions certainly had that effect. And furthermore . . ."

Seemingly oblivious to her husband's continuing speech, or his angry glare, the smiling hostess turned to her guests and began again, "You must excuse the Ambassador. He's just riding his hobby horse. The Christ story is his pet subject," she explained in her sweetest tone, "and the role Pontius Pilate played in the Christ story is his pet theory. He will talk about it to anyone."

Her laughter tinkled as the Ambassador fumed. "I don't know why he hasn't written a book about it himself," she continued. "After all, it seems they will publish *anything* these days."

If possible, the silence around the table intensified.

Perhaps, suddenly sensing awkwardness, the ninny glanced around and—still smiling—launched into a subject even more uncomfortable for Wallace.

"Now, do tell us please, *dear* Governor, about your days in the Wild West. Did you have marvelous adventures? Wasn't controlling the affairs of an entire Territory exciting?"

If only that *had been true! "Affairs controlling him" had been more like it.*

New Mexico had meant nothing but three years of anger and frustration. Such a disaster! And so unfair, after he had nearly lived down those accusations of incompetence during the War.

He had tried *so* hard to govern well, but everything just seemed *different* in *that place.* As he had written Susan, "All calculations based on our experiences elsewhere fail in New Mexico."

The former general had started his governorship with so many hopes and expectations for the new land. Hopes and expectations quashed at every turn by the perverse nature of the Territory and everyone in it.

Machinations of the Santa Fe Ring—that loose coalition of powerful businessmen, unscrupulous politicians, conniving lawyers, and weaseling judges—blocked his good intentions at every turn, as if the snail-like pace of progress among the "Mexican" population wasn't infuriating enough. Feelings of impotence had only grown in the face of increasing violence, deceit, and corruption.

And not the genteel kind of corruption every governor expects to encounter. Why, he himself had not been averse to pursuing an advantageous mining investment, a slightly questionable land transaction here or there, or an occasional reward for granting a favored contract.

But the Santa Fe Ring pushed everything to horrid extremes. And the violence they supported! So many good men had died during the Lincoln County War, not to mention all the bad ones.

The former governor shook his head as he thought of his attempts to restore law and order to that almost-lawless portion of the Territory, down in southern New Mexico.

Susan understood. She knew how difficult those years had been for him. She had never made a secret of her own dislike of Santa Fe either, and of the whole Territory for that matter. Why, she once wrote their son that the United States should have another war with Old Mexico to make her take back New Mexico.

In spite of his entreaties, most of the time Susan had refused to remain in the Territory, which left him alone among a sea of strangers with strange ways, foreigners really, in addition to those scheming businessmen and politicians.

He had done the best he could, but each month brought new disasters, escalating violence, and increased rumblings of dissatisfaction from Washington.

Thank goodness, the limited demands on his time in that slow-paced world had allowed him to complete *Ben Hur*. And, thank goodness, his novel had made such a striking impression on President Garfield. And—most especially—thank *goodness*, the President had finalized his appointment to the Ottoman Empire before a deranged assassin put a bullet in the poor man's spine.

What a glorious deliverance! Constantinople, and the East! Surely, Providence was rewarding him for bringing his Tale of the Christ to the masses.

"Governor, *Governor*," the ninny insisted. "You simply must share some of your adventures with us."

In spite of his distaste for the subject, the Governor obliged by beginning an account of his life on the frontier.

"Were you really in a war out there?" asked one dinner guest.

"They did call it the Lincoln County War, but it was actually just a drawn-out fight between two competing factions for economic control of the area. But then," he mused, "aren't most wars?"

"Tell us how it got started," urged another guest farther down the table as he leaned forward to see Wallace better.

What could he say? How to explain such a complicated conflict without boring everyone?

"Two Irishmen, Lawrence Murphy and James Dolan, held all the government contracts to supply beef and other foodstuffs to the Army post of Fort Stanton and the nearby Mescalero Apache Reservation. Backed by the powerful Santa Fe Ring, they also ran a mercantile business that monopolized trade with most settlers in the area. Then, English newcomer John Tunstall joined with lawyer Alexander McSween and "The Cattle King of the Pecos," John Chisum, to challenge their control."

"Ah, the English and the Irish, at it again."

"Perhaps," reflected Wallace. "Certainly as bloody—and as futile. Each faction brought in a frightening array of gunfighters to back its position. Many died, including several of the principals, and in the end, no one emerged a clear winner, except maybe a few members of the Santa Fe Ring who fattened their purses."

"Now Governor," chided the ninny. "We want to hear adventures, not philosophizing."

Appropriately chastised, Wallace switched to recounting some of the more dramatic events of that conflict: the murder of young Tunstall, the daylight ambush of Sheriff Brady on the streets of Lincoln, the deadly five-day siege at McSween's adobe *hacienda*.

Wallace could see the company hanging on his every word. His mood brightened. *I really am quite a storyteller, aren't I?* he thought.

And, after all, there *had* been some exciting times. He had even been able to take a personal role in some of the action.

There in Lincoln County, mixing with the desperados, walking the dusty streets where deadly shootouts had taken place just the year before, he felt so alive, a hero leading an epic battle against the forces of evil.

Susan had even accompanied him down there on one trip. Wallace always had to chuckle to himself when he recalled her reaction. "I did not believe anything could make me think well of Santa Fe," she remarked, "but this hideous spot does." She *really* detested southern New Mexico.

However, those visits to Lincoln County had thrilled the Governor himself, especially his secret late-night meeting with that young outlaw William Bonney, when they struck their clandestine bargain and plotted their strategy.

Bonney had agreed to submit to a staged arrest so he could testify before a grand jury about the murder of lawyer Huston Chapman on the streets of Lincoln. He would also appear at the military Court of Inquiry into Colonel Dudley's illegal actions during the five-day siege. Exactly what Wallace wanted!

You had to admit that Billy Bonney had courage, especially for someone so young. Going up against desperate killers and corrupt lawmen, not to mention the military—and all alone, too.

Governor Wallace had delighted at the prospect of bringing those evil-doers to justice. And all he had to do was promise Bonney a pardon.

Of course, those events had hardly turned out as planned either. Chapman's vicious murderers, finally indicted by the grand jury? They simply saddled up and rode out of the Territory.

And the Court of Inquiry? The fools—or more likely, Colonel Dudley's corrupt buddies—completely ignored all of

Wallace's efforts to bring out the truth about Dudley's illegal use of troops to support the Santa Fe Ring's favored faction during that five-day siege.

More hopes crushed.

But he didn't go into that story for his fellow dinner guests. And he certainly didn't bring up the young gunman whose face kept flashing before him.

That's why the ninny's next question startled him so. "Did you become friendly with any of those colorful gun fighters?"

"No! Certainly not!" Her hurt expression suggested that he had perhaps responded too sharply.

And his response did not strictly represent the truth. There had been several actually, but especially the one whose image had been haunting him all evening.

William Bonney was certainly an intriguing youngster. No one knew where he came from. Some said New York City. As far as Wallace could tell, he was really just some drifting cow hand—a small time rustler maybe—good with a gun.

And, that, he certainly was—good with a gun. Wallace had seen it for himself.

After Bonney's arranged arrest, the sheriff had confined the popular young outlaw in Juan Peron's small store, right next door to Governor Wallace's own lodgings, rather than subject him to Lincoln County's dank, poorly designed hole-in-the-ground of a jail.

Amazingly, deputies had even allowed the young man to put on an impromptu demonstration of his gun-handling skills one afternoon. Wallace had watched as the youngster twirled his pistols, then unerringly shattered bottle after bottle, even those tossed into the air.

Afterward he asked the boy about his skills.

"I practice whenever I get the chance—and whenever I have money for cartridges."

"Your aim seems uncanny."

"Well, sir, I noticed a long time ago that when a man points his finger at something, his aim is usually dead on. I just point with my pistol and it works like pointing with my finger. Anyone can do it, sir, even you," he said with a mischievous grin.

The youngster clearly had audacity— and charm. Wallace had felt the attraction himself. Quick-witted, knowledgeable, well-spoken, quite a surprise for an outlaw.

All the locals loved him, maybe because he laughed and joked with them in their native tongue. "Billy the Kid" they called him, *El Chivito* in Spanish—a young goat, but maybe a rascally one.

Not a bad looking fellow either, with his slim wiry build, fair complexion, and striking blue eyes. Perhaps his front teeth did stick out a bit, but that certainly didn't stop the *señoritas* from chasing after him. And their smiling *mamas* referred to him affectionately as *Bilito,* "little Billy."

Why, one evening the Governor heard guitar music and singing coming from outside his window and went to investigate. What did he discover? The townspeople gathered around Juan Peron's store serenading their beloved desperado!

But Wallace certainly wasn't going to regale the dinner guests with stories of that outlaw. The insignificant wretch had already received far too much attention. Time for him to fade from everyone's memory, especially Wallace's.

Why, then, couldn't the governor get the youngster out of his thoughts that night?

The company fell silent once more.

"Interesting stories, Governor Wallace, interesting stories," harrumphed the Ambassador. "Now, as I was saying, about Pontius Pilate . . ." and the Ambassador took off again.

Much later, after the fireworks, Wallace tossed and turned in his elegant but stifling bed chamber. Distant church bells tolled each successive quarter-hour as he reviewed events of the evening.

First, the Ambassador's pontification. Interesting after all, to give Pontius Pilate credit for setting fateful events in motion. Without his actions, there would have been no story, according to the Ambassador. Pilate bore responsibility for everything that followed, everything that created the story of the Christ, everything that made Jesus of Nazareth memorable.

Wallace wondered if that thought had ever occurred to Pilate himself. Surely, no. Such a man could never have admitted to himself that a cowardly action on his part had led to such fame for someone who, in his view, was merely an insignificant miscreant.

And, after all, wasn't that view a bit extreme?

Wallace re-examined Pontius Pilate's role in the story. Jerusalem, the Passover holiday, the most joyous event of the Jewish calendar, celebrating the deliverance of the Jews from bondage in Egypt.

When Roman soldiers arrested Jesus for speaking against the Roman Empire, they brought him before Pontius Pilate, Governor of the Province.

Pilate could easily have released Jesus. He wanted to let him go. He argued for release. But powerful men demanded punishment. What might they do to Pilate's career and his reputation if he defied them? The Roman administrator struggled mightily with the dilemma.

Finally he hit upon a safe solution. He would pass the decision on to the people. Let them be the jury. Let them condemn or release Jesus.

He did just that, and the Crucifixion followed, then the Resurrection, and thus began the Greatest Story Ever Told. Jesus' fame spread worldwide, down through the centuries. Everyone hears the story from childhood, all thanks to Pontius Pilate, all because he feared to release a minor troublemaker.

Yes, an interesting theory, but why did the Ambassador need to go on and on about it? And why does that eerie feeling keep arising?

Wallace's thoughts turned once more to New Mexico. Was it somehow connected with that distressing feeling? Even as he tangled himself in the suffocating bedclothes, longing for sleep, or at least, for relief from the July Paris heat, unease dogged him, along with increasingly intrusive thoughts of the outlaw Billy Bonney.

How odd. Why him? Why tonight?

He had successfully put the young man out of his mind for months now. Why did these images so fill his head tonight? And why was the boy wearing such a sad expression instead of his usual cheerful grin?

Perhaps the Ambassador's talk of Jesus of Nazareth and Pontius Pilate had triggered some association?

No! No connection!

Still, Billy Bonney wouldn't go away. Almost unwillingly, the Governor reviewed his own actions regarding the pardon, for at least the hundredth time—actions that sometimes felt like another failure, a personal failure, a moral failure.

No. He had done what he had to do.

As he told the reporter, "I can't see how a fellow like him should expect any clemency from me."

Yet in his heart, he knew why the young desperado would expect clemency. There had been a promise, hadn't there?

Still, just because Billy Bonney kept his part of the bargain and testified before the grand jury and, later, the Court of Inquiry, that was no reason for Wallace to sacrifice his own career for a two-bit hoodlum.

If truth be told, he could easily have pardoned the young desperado. After all, wasn't the boy's crime more like shooting an enemy soldier in wartime, instead of an actual murder?

He had pardoned nearly all the others for their Lincoln County killings. No one else had been prosecuted, only the Kid. Bonney had a point when he complained to a newspaperman about being singled out, "At least 200 men have been killed in Lincoln County during the past three years. I did not kill them all."

But those lawyers and judges—Santa Fe Ring members all—had wanted so badly to see the Kid hang! Especially District Attorney Rynerson, quite an intimidating man, nearly seven feet tall, with a monstrously bushy beard. He'd been most adamant about denying the pardon.

What gave that hairy giant cause to be so vindictive? Hadn't he himself once murdered the Chief Justice of the Territorial Supreme Court and gone scot-free with a dubious claim of self-defense—and a lawyer from the Santa Fe Ring?

Why did those hounds demand the Kid's hide? To make an example of him for opposing their grip on the Territory? Who knows? But those powerful lawyers and judges had the ear of the President. Why risk retaliation? They could easily have destroyed his political career.

In the face of that threat, he certainly couldn't let the Kid go free. No, it was best to let others decide. No, no pardon. Instead, a decision by a jury of his peers. The perfect solution. He could wash his hands of the whole affair. And that would be the end of it. One way or another, guilty or innocent, the insignificant young man would soon be forgotten.

Even *that* didn't quite work out as he had hoped. Yes, the trial had gone forward. Yes, the jury had found him guilty. Yes, the judge had sentenced him to hang. Nothing unusual about that out West. The story was over. The youngster's name had begun to fade from memory.

But then—the spectacular escape! Shackled hand and foot, the Kid had managed to shoot two deputies and make a daring ride through the mountains to freedom. Newspapers went wild.

Even with all that, the sensation only lasted a few days. Other stories replaced it. People were starting to forget again.

What would have happened if he had pardoned the Kid?

If Bonney had never stood trial for murder, had never been sentenced to hang, had never made that daring escape killing those two deputies, he would simply have gone back to being the obscure cattle rustler he had always been.

Really though, the governor told himself, there was probably no difference in the final outcome for Bonney. The young hoodlum had likely high-tailed it down to Old Mexico by now, never to be heard from again.

The Kid would probably live out his days, however few or many, in some nondescript village south of the border, chasing more *señoritas* and swilling tequila, forgotten forever. The same as if he had received the pardon.

But the difference for Wallace was enormous. What if he had stirred up the displeasure of the Santa Fe Ring? Would President Garfield still have appointed him Minister to the Ottoman Empire? Unlikely.

Instead, he had done what the situation demanded, and was now on his way to Constantinople. A happy ending for everyone, really—except those two dead deputies, of course.

Truly, no reason to think about the Kid ever again. Interest had already died down once more. Soon, nobody would even remember that bucktoothed young tough from the New Mexico desert. He would fade into the shadows of history, forgotten, one more nobody.

With that satisfying thought, Lew Wallace finally drifted off to sleep.

Hissing steam and cries of hawkers filled the warm morning air. Governor Wallace and his wife stood on the station platform preparing to board the train that would carry them on to Constantinople.

At the last minute, the Ambassador arrived, puffing mightily. "Sorry to be late, but I was waiting for the latest news about President Garfield's condition. Not good, I'm afraid, even after all this time. He still lives, but hopes for his recovery are mixed. Doctors are trying all sorts of procedures, but results are disappointing."

Pausing to catch his breath, the Ambassador then added, "The telegraph brought some other news that might interest you, Governor. News from New Mexico. A sheriff named Pat Garrett killed that notorious outlaw Billy the Kid. Shot him in the dark in somebody's bedroom. Happened on the fourteenth, that night we were watching the fireworks."

Wallace stared as the Ambassador continued, "I can't imagine how some penny-ante outlaw could even merit mention on the same telegraph wire as the President of the United States."

DEAD OR ALIVE ?

The Ambassador shook his head sadly. "From what the newspapers say, he was just some insignificant hired thug before they decided to try him for murder. Then he cheated the hangman by making that daring escape. All that's what captured the world's attention, I suppose. Turned a forgettable nobody into news. And now, we hear nothing but 'Billy the Kid, Billy the Kid, Billy the Kid' . . . Humph! I wonder who we have to thank for *that!*"

Governor Wallace could only generate a wan smile as he helped Susan up into the train.

Won't that infernal youngster ever go away?

Then a comforting revelation struck him. *Of course he will! He's dead now. Gone. End of story. Another couple of weeks and everyone will forget him forever. No one will even remember his name, and I'll never have to hear it again, or think about . . . any of that.*

The Minister Plenipotentiary's smile took on a glow of pleasure as the train began its journey eastward.

Ah . . . freedom.

Lew Wallace

From *The Leading Facts of New Mexican History, vol 2.*
by Ralph Emerson Twitchell.
Cedar Rapids, Iowa: Torch Press, 1912.

The Best Escape

*(A comment by Hercule Poirot about
the perfect murder inspired this story)*

"GRANDPA! GRANDPA! Tell us about Billy the Kid's escape again!" clamored the two young boys.

"Do you mean when he shot his way out of the burning house during the five-day-siege?"

"No Grandpa, his best escape!"

"Do you mean when he broke out of the Lincoln County jail, shackled hand-and-foot, and rode across the mountains to freedom?" teased the old man.

"No, Grandpa! You know! His *best* escape! The one where he fooled Sheriff Pat Garrett and lived happily ever after."

The youngsters sprawled themselves in front of their grandfather's porch chair as dust devils swirled over the scorched New Mexico landscape.

The old man settled himself as comfortably as he could. Darned rheumatism always made it hard.

"Whew, it's hot! Wouldn't it be nice to have one of those electrical fans to cool us off? Course, I don't suppose it would do us much good out here on the ranch with no electricity," he chuckled. "Oh well, maybe someday . . ."

Then he began.

Now, Billy the Kid was a dashing young cowboy, with wavy brown hair and bright blue eyes, even though he used to get teased some because of the way his front teeth stuck out. "He's so bucktoothed he could bite a pumpkin through a picket fence," other young toughs would taunt him.

The *señoritas* didn't mind though. That youngster could charm the stripes off a tiger and dance the shoes off a goose. They say he had a *querida*—that's a sweetheart, you know—in every village.

Now, don't think Billy was just any old cowhand. He was smart and he had some education. He loved reading dime novels and he always read the newspaper whenever he could get it. He might have become a newspaper writer himself, or maybe even a lawyer, if he'd had half a chance.

But Billy had a hard life growing up. He never knew his father and his mother died when he was only fourteen. Billy was pretty much on his own after that. He had to learn to live in the rough world on the New Mexico frontier.

Things weren't like they are today. Back then, men had to be able to fight for every scrap they could grab.

Well, Billy managed as best he could. He didn't always follow the law and he did do some mighty bad things, although he did some mighty good ones too. Mostly, he just hoped to find a nice *señorita* and make a good life for himself, and for her and some children, on a quiet New Mexico ranch.

You see, even though he was a blue-eyed Anglo, he had learned to talk Spanish as a boy in Santa Fe. He loved the Mexican way of living. He made so many friends among the Mexican families around the town of Lincoln, down there in the southern part of the Territory, that most all of them welcomed him into their homes, any time of day or night. Some even hid him from the law when he was on the run.

Now, Billy got involved in what they called a "war" there in Lincoln County. Two different rings of rich businessmen were fighting over who would get all the contracts to supply beef to the army post and to the Mescalero Reservation, and who would sell goods to the settlers.

Each side started bringing in hired guns for protection, and to devil the other side. Lots of fighting and killing got started.

Billy was pretty good with a gun himself and, before long, he joined up with one of the sides. His boss, a young Englishman, took a fancy to him, and Billy got to looking on that boss almost like the father he never knew.

When gunmen from the other side murdered the Englishman, Billy vowed revenge. The war kept going on and more men died on each side, some in fair fights and some in ambushes—or in out-and-out cold-blooded killings.

Many of the gunfighters, including Billy, got accused of murder. The Governor pardoned most of them—but not Billy—just to put an end to the violence. When the fighting finally died down, two hundred men had died, and nothing much was settled.

With no reason to stay in Lincoln County, Billy and several of his pals drifted on over east to the high plains near Fort Sumner and set up a small cattle operation for themselves.

Cattle ranching was different back then, too. There were no fenced pastures or barbed wire. In those days, running cattle often meant rounding up wandering strays to add to the herd.

Now, some of those strays weren't always exactly strays, but nobody paid much attention to such details. It seemed like everybody was doing it.

Billy and his pals started making a fair living over there. Life got pretty tame for a while. But powerful men in Santa Fe still hated Billy from the Lincoln County War, cause he had shot their sheriff. Big cattle ranchers got tired of his rustling, even if it was really just a nuisance to them more than anything else.

They all finally got together and convinced Governor Wallace to put a $500 bounty on his head. Billy the Kid: Wanted Dead or Alive.

Those powerful men even got one of Billy's old running buddies from Fort Sumner named Pat Garrett elected Sheriff of

Lincoln County. His job was to bring Billy in, and he did just that.

They tried Billy for the murder of that sheriff and sentenced him to hang, but he escaped, killing two of Pat's deputies in the process. Everybody knows that story.

Now one deputy was a mean SOB. Most people thought he needed killing anyway. But the other one was a good man. Yep, Billy always felt bad about killing Deputy Bell. But when it came down to life and death, Billy chose life, even if it meant death for a good man.

After his escape, everybody figured Billy had left the Territory, figured he was hiding out down in Mexico. But they were wrong.

Billy went back to Fort Sumner. He had plenty of friends there, and one special lady he couldn't leave behind—not to mention a few others who thought they were his chosen *querida*. Billy did enjoy the company of young ladies!

Why, even Paulita Maxwell, the little sister of Pete Maxwell who owned most of Fort Sumner and everything around it, had enjoyed Billy's attentions from time to time. She'd even started telling all sorts of romance stories about her and Billy to anybody who would listen. That girl sure knew

what she wanted—and she expected to get it
. . . oh yes . . .

Billy could charm the older ones too.
Deluvina, was one of those. She had worked
as a servant for Pete's family since she was
little. That woman would do *anything* for
Billy. She treated him like her favorite son,
although I think she was really kind of sweet
on him in a different way herself.

Surprisingly enough, even the men—
including Pete—liked Billy, probably because of his daring ways and his loyalty to
his friends. Things like that counted a lot in
those rough and tumble days.

Of course, Pat Garrett went looking
for Billy again after his escape. It didn't take
him long to track Billy to their old stomping
grounds in Fort Sumner.

Pat figured their old buddy Pete, or
Don Pedro as the locals called him, might
know something so he headed straight for
Pete's big hacienda.

It was late evening when he and his
posse arrived. He stationed his two armed
deputies on the porch, under the *portal*,
while he went to Pete's bedroom to wake
him up and ask about Billy.

What Pat didn't know was that Billy
was making his own visit to Pete's hacienda

that night. You see, his special lady lived in part of Pete's sprawling compound.

Pretty soon, Billy, who had missed dinner to come calling, started getting hungry. "Go ask Juan to fix you some food. I'm sure he's still there in the kitchen," suggested his dark-eyed beauty.

Billy hurriedly buttoned up and slipped across the moonlit yard to the kitchen. There, the lingering odor of fried onions made his mouth water and his stomach rumble.

The cook was happy to help. "Can you see that beef quarter hanging under the *portal* by Don Pedro's bedroom? Go cut you a steak and I'll fry it up for you. I know he won't mind."

Billy grabbed a butcher knife and was heading for the beef when the sight of two men in the shadows spooked him. He ducked through the open door into Pete's bedroom.

Pat, who was sitting on Pete's bed by that time, didn't recognize the man coming toward him, but pulled his pistol from its holster anyway.

Billy couldn't see much in the darkened bedroom. Still, he sensed that Pete was not alone. "*Quien es?* Who is it?" he called urgently.

Before Pete could answer, two pistol shots exploded.

Billy fell to the floor.

Now, ole Pat always was a terrible shot, even in broad daylight. There in that dim bedroom, he sent one bullet way over Billy's head, while the other just grazed his skull.

I don't know whether that bullet knocked Billy out or he hit his head ducking and scrambling for cover but he ended up spread-eagle on the floor unconscious.

Not that Pat would have known. He and Pete, who by now had bolted out of bed, dragging the tangled bedclothes behind him, were too busy fighting each other to be the first one out the door.

Did I tell you, they took to calling Pete "Don Chootme" after that, cause of what he was yelling when he came blasting through the door? I don't suppose anyone called him that to his face though, not if he wanted to keep his job.

Anyway, the sound of shots brought people running. The cook and servants, including Deluvina, soon joined ranch hands and neighbors—mostly friends of Billy—in front of the moonlit porch.

"I shot Billy the Kid! I shot Billy the Kid!" spluttered Pat to the gathering crowd.

"Nah, that wasn't Billy," spoke up one deputy. "You shot the wrong man."

"No, I shot Billy!" insisted Pat. "I recognized his voice!"

Despite the doubt, nobody wanted to go back inside the bedroom to check, least of all Pat. He was afraid Billy was just waiting in there to kill him.

Pete finally pulled himself together enough to fetch a candle. He lit it with shaking hands and cautiously held it up to the open bedroom window. In its flickering light, they could make out a motionless figure stretched out on the floor.

While others stood muttering among themselves, Deluvina grabbed the candle from Pete and marched into the bedroom. Only Billy's friend Chuy followed her in.

There lay Billy on the floor—dead.

Or was he? Was that a faint rising of his chest? His arm moved. Deluvina drew a quick breath. Then she bent down and gently shook the boy's shoulder.

Billy's eyes blinked open. He struggled to rise.

"No!" whispered Deluvina, slowly pressing him back to the floor. "Lie still! Be quiet!"

Emotions played across her shadowy face. "*Bilito*, this is your chance to be free. That coward Garrett thinks he killed you but he's too scared to come back in here to see for sure. Do what I tell you and you'll be through with him forever."

"I don't know . . ."

"Think about it, Billy. Look at you. You're half dressed. You're not even wearing boots. Just what were you doing here to-night?"

"Me? . . . I was visiting someone."

"Paulita?"

"Well, uh . . . no."

"No. I didn't think so. You *better* play dead then. If Paulita finds out you were here with someone else, she'll kill you her-self. You know she's been telling everybody, including her brother, that you two are get-ting married. She means to make that hap-pen. Do what I say and you'll be free from her hooks as well."

Billy's eyes fixed on the servant's tense face. Maybe what she was saying made sense. But could it work? Slowly he nodded, as a boyish, bucktoothed grin snuck across his face.

"*Bilito*, you lie right here. Don't move and don't make a sound."

"Chuy, don't say a word but come with me," directed Deluvina, rising. "Just go along with whatever I do."

Deluvina burst from the bedroom, hurling the candle at Pat Garrett's feet. "Murderer! *Asesino!*" she screamed as she struck wildly at the lanky lawman, her blows barely reaching his shoulders. "You've killed my *Bilito!*"

Gasps came from the still-gathering crowd. Chuy caught at Deluvina's flailing arms and made a show of soothing her cries and sobs. As he led her off into the darkness, voices in the crowd grew louder. Accusations rang out.

Pat glanced back and forth between his deputies and the hostile faces surrounding them. The three lawmen edged closer together. "Pete, have you got a safe place for us?" Pat croaked.

"Come with me," Pete mumbled, still shaken. He led them to an empty bedroom with a solid wooden door blocking its only entrance. "You'll be fine in here."

Back outside, Chuy had returned to the porch. He called to several of Billy's other friends. "Joseph, Vicente, help me carry Billy's body over to the carpenter shop. We'll lay him out there while we get to work on a coffin."

Once in the bedroom, with the situation quickly explained to them, all agreed to help with Deluvina's plan. Grabbing arms and legs, they hustled the "body" out through the milling crowd to the carpenter shop across the dusty yard.

Chuy closed the door behind them to shut out curious eyes. So far, everything was working beautifully.

Deluvina waited inside. Under her direction, they laid out the "dead" outlaw on an old carpenter's bench.

Then they noticed a problem. A trickle of blood continued to flow from the wound on Billy's scalp. Now, corpses shouldn't keep bleeding, you know, so Deluvina hurried to her room and found a potion among her store of native medicines to put a stop to that. One problem solved.

The next difficulty was deciding whether or not to tell Pete the truth. Billy argued—quietly, of course—for not including him in the plot.

Deluvina finally convinced him otherwise. "Somebody will surely let something slip someday and if Pete finds out we tricked him, will he be mad! Who knows what he'll do! But if we tell him now, I think he'll help, if for no other reason than to stop Paulita from chasing after you. You know, Billy, even though he likes you, he doesn't fancy you as a brother-in-law."

The group elected Deluvina to explain the situation to her employer. She soon returned with the good news that Pete would go along with their plan. She even brought back a clean shirt he had donated to dress Billy in for the wake.

Deluvina also brought a young lady named Manuela back with her, whose joy at finding Billy alive was quite touching and maybe a little embarrassing. For a few minutes, their hugging and kissing was just like something out of a romance novel. All that made it pretty clear that she was the *querida* Billy had come to see.

Once Manuela understood what had happened in Pete's bedroom, the group had trouble keeping her from going after Pat. Her dark eyes flashed with anger. "How could he just shoot you like that? You weren't even carrying a pistol. What kind of coward shoots an unarmed man in the dark?"

"Oh, Billy will have been carrying a pistol, maybe two, before the telling is all over, just you hide and watch," muttered Chuy.

When they finally got Manuela settled down, Joseph opened the door of the carpenter shop for all to view.

Deluvina had arranged the scene beautifully. Billy, in his clean white shirt, lay on the bench, eyes closed and hands folded over his chest. A single candle burned by his head—you wouldn't want too much light in there, you know.

The older woman sat at one end of the bench, while the younger one sat at the other end, both with their covered heads bowed in prayer. Chuy and Vicente stood off to the side.

Sobs occasionally escaped from the handkerchief Manuela held to her lips, especially when she noticed a mourner in the doorway. That's where Joseph managed to stop the sad and the curious "in respect for the women's grief."

Deluvina and Manuela maintained their vigil throughout the night, occasionally having to prod Billy awake. After all, a snoring corpse is even more suspicious than a bleeding one.

Billy worried some that Paulita would want to sit up with his body as well, but Deluvina assured him that wouldn't be a problem. She explained that while she was out looking for Pete, she had stopped in Paulita's bedroom to wake the sleeping girl.

After Paulita went through her expected fits of screaming and fainting at news of Billy's death, Deluvina managed to mention Billy's puzzling half-dressed state, and added that poor distraught Manuela had already joined the vigil for him in the carpenter shop.

The faithful servant silently congratulated herself as she watched Paulita's showy grief turn to fury at the thought of Billy's final moments in the arms of a rival. No, Paulita would not be joining the vigil.

In fact, I'm not even sure Paulita showed up at the funeral, although over time her version of her love affair with Billy grew more and more dramatic. Soon, Billy was tragically cut down on the very eve of their wedding.

Deluvina's worry that night centered more on whether Pat Garrett would want to examine Billy's body. Fortunately, that never became a problem either.

Pat and his deputies were so scared of Billy's friends coming after them that they stayed holed up in that spare bedroom all night, taking turns guarding the door. At first light, they hightailed it back to Lincoln.

Pat had seen enough of Billy to last him a lifetime.

The conspirators still had another worry though: the coroner's jury. Even on New Mexico's wild frontier, a coroner's jury always looked into every killing to figure out exactly what had happened. The jury then filed an official report with Territorial offices in Santa Fe. How could Deluvina and the others handle a coroner's jury?

Fortunately, Pat solved that problem for them. Before he took off for Lincoln, he stopped in at Pete's bedroom one more time to hand him a paper.

On that paper, Pat had written out the whole coroner's jury report himself, saying how the jury had examined the body and talked to witnesses and declared the killing a justifiable homicide. He even added a part about how the whole community owed Sheriff Pat Garrett its gratitude for killing Billy and how he deserved a reward for his brave act.

Pat told Pete to round up some men to sign the paper as the coroner's jury, so he could get that reward. I guess Pete did it, cause no real coroner's jury ever came looking for Billy's body.

During the night, Chuy had hammered a coffin together from rough pine boards. When he finished, he set it up in the middle of the carpenter shop, carefully nailed shut of course.

Deluvina slipped Billy out the back way just before dawn and hid him in one of the outbuildings.

Then, while Manuela and Joseph stayed with the coffin, Chuy and Vicente headed out to the old military cemetery to dig a grave. Soldiers from the abandoned fort were buried there, as well as Pete's daddy, old Lucien Maxwell. Two of Billy's best buddies lay there too, right next to each other, both killed by Pat Garrett and his posses.

Soon after dawn, streams of local folks began to come by the carpenter shop to pay their respects. By noontime, they had covered that pine box with bunches of those little purple flowers and the sweet-smelling wild pink roses that grow everywhere.

Once the heat of the day had passed, Vicente hitched up his mule to his wood-hauling wagon and brought it around to the carpenter shop. Joseph and Chuy helped him load the coffin onto the wagon for the trip to the cemetery.

"Grandpa, how did they make it seem like there was a body in he coffin?" asked the younger boy, knowing the answer by heart.

"I don't know for sure, son, but that beef quarter hanging by Pete's bedroom door disappeared mighty mysteriously sometime in the night. From what I heard, Joseph always swore they buried it in Billy's place, but then, that old cowhand never was one to let the truth get in the way of a good story."

Nearly the whole population of Fort Sumner followed Vicente's wagon to the cemetery for the funeral. Some say Billy even joined the procession, but I don't think Deluvina would have let him take that risk, no matter how well disguised he was. He sure would have enjoyed attending his own funeral, though.

Quite a funeral it was too! First came the preaching in English, then the praying in Spanish. Finally, six or eight of Billy's friends spoke nice words about him while the women stood around crying softly.

Most of the men took turns throwing a shovelful or two of dirt into the grave until it was filled. Then Chuy set up a rough wooden cross on top.

Afterward, the crowd headed back home by twos and threes, all except Deluvina who stayed on, almost till dark. I don't know if that was for show or if she really was saying her last goodbyes to her *Bilito*.

You know, after all these years, Deluvina still puts wildflowers on Billy's grave every summer—to keep up the pretence, I guess, although maybe the flowers mean more to her than just a way to fool people.

Anyway, Billy did get away to lead a new life, although he always kept in touch with his friends in round-about ways. And he did marry his *querida*.

Together, they made a good life for themselves on their own little New Mexico ranch. They both worked hard and raised lots of cattle—and lively sons and beautiful daughters—and they all lived happily ever after.

Pat Garrett went on to collect his $500, and more, from all New Mexico's grateful citizens. He became the most famous lawman in all the Territory, and maybe all the West, for a little while at least. He even wrote a book about how he had killed the notorious outlaw, Billy the Kid. Pat went to his grave—shot in the back himself under mysterious circumstances—believing he was the hero of his own story.

Paulita never knew the truth either. But she sure seemed to get over her tragic romance quickly enough and marry someone else. Soon, they had a fine son—maybe too soon—but you boys never mind about that. Still, some people said he looked a lot like Billy . . .

Anyway, the point is that everyone kept the secret, although a few rumors still go around from time to time. Mostly, they say that Pat shot the wrong man, and then he and his deputies covered up his mistake. Many thought he really shot one of Pete Maxwell's cowhands.

Others said that the whole thing was just a set-up, that Billy and Pat, being old buddies, had cooked it up together to get Pat the reward and to get Billy a new chance in life.

"Wouldn't that have been a good way to escape, Grandpa? If Billy and Pat had fixed it up between themselves?"

"Sure son, that would have been a *good* escape, but Billy found the *best* escape. Do you know what the best escape is?"

"Tell us, Grandpa, tell us!" the boys urged as they always did when he came to this part of the story.

"The best escape," continued the old man, dropping his voice after making a show of glancing over both shoulders, "is when they don't even know you're gone."

The screen door banged noisily behind a young woman as she stepped out onto the dusty porch. "Papa! There you go again! I've told you and told you. Don't be filling their heads with your nonsense."

The old man glanced up at her, then down at the floor. How her dark eyes flashed when she was angry—just like her mother's always had.

"Why do you make up such stories? Everybody knows Pat Garrett killed Billy the Kid and buried him down there at Fort Sumner!"

"Yes Darlin'," the old man responded quietly, his eyes still on the floor.

But his blue eyes twinkled as a familiar bucktoothed grin stole across his now-wrinkled face.

And dust devils swirled across distant fields under the scorching New Mexico sun.

Pat Garrett

From *The Authentic Life of Billy, the Kid*
by Pat Garrett.
Santa Fe: New Mexico Printing and Publishing Company,
1882.

BONUS
SELECTION

Killing Billy the Kid

from

The Authentic Life of Billy, the Kid
by Sheriff Pat Garrett
Santa Fe: New Mexico Printing and
Publishing Company, 1882

*In his 1882 biography of Billy the Kid, Pat
Garrett described the death of the outlaw at
Fort Sumner, New Mexico, as follows:*

[DEPUTY] POE'S APPEARANCE at Sumner had
excited no particular observation, and he
had gleaned no news there. [Rancher
Milnor] Rudolph thought, from all
indications, that the Kid was about; and yet,
at times, he doubted. His cause for doubt
seemed to be based on no evidence except
the fact that the Kid was no fool, and no
man in his senses, under the circumstances,
would brave such danger.

I then concluded to go and have a
talk with Peter Maxwell, Esq., in whom I felt
sure I could rely.

DEAD OR ALIVE ?

We had ridden to within a short distance of Maxwell's grounds when we found a man in camp and stopped. To Poe's great surprise, he recognized in the camper an old friend and former partner, in Texas, named Jacobs.

We unsaddled here, got some coffee, and, on foot, entered an orchard which runs from this point down to a row of old buildings, some of them occupied by Mexicans, not more than sixty yards from Maxwell's house.

We approached these houses cautiously, and when within ear shot, heard the sound of voices conversing in Spanish. We concealed ourselves quickly and listened; but the distance was too great to hear words, or even distinguish voices.

Soon a man arose from the ground, in full view, but too far away to recognize. He wore a broad-brimmed hat, a dark vest and pants, and was in his shirt sleeves. With a few words, which fell like a murmur on our ears, he went to the fence, jumped it, and walked down towards Maxwell's house.

Little as we then suspected it, this man was the Kid. We learned, subsequently, that, when he left his companions that night, he went to the house of a Mexican friend, pulled off his hat and boots, threw himself on a bed, and commenced reading a newspaper.

He soon, however, hailed his friend, who was sleeping in the room, told him to get up and make some coffee, adding:

—"Give me a butcher knife and I will go over to Pete's and get some beef; I'm hungry."

The Mexican arose, handed him the knife, and the Kid, hatless and in his stocking-feet, started to Maxwell's, which was but a few steps distant.

When the Kid, by me unrecognized, left the orchard, I motioned to my companions, and we cautiously retreated a short distance, and, to avoid the persons whom we had heard at the houses, took another route, approaching Maxwell's house from the opposite direction.

When we reached the porch in front of the building, I left Poe and [Deputy] McKinney at the end of the porch, about twenty feet from the door of Pete's room, and went in.

It was near midnight and Pete was in bed. I walked to the head of the bed and sat down on it, beside him, near the pillow. I asked him as to the whereabouts of the Kid. He said that the Kid had certainly been about, but he did not know whether he had left or not.

At that moment a man sprang quickly into the door, looking back, and called twice in Spanish, "Who comes there?"

No one replied and he came on in. He was bareheaded. From his step I could perceive he was either barefooted or in his stocking-feet, and held a revolver in his right hand and a butcher knife in his left.

He came directly towards me. Before he reached the bed, I whispered: "Who is it, Pete?" but received no reply for a moment.

It struck me that it might be Pete's brother-in-law, Manuel Abreu, who had seen Poe and McKinney, and wanted to know their business.

The intruder came close to me, leaned both hands on the bed, his right hand almost touching my knee, and asked, in a low tone:

—"Who are they Pete?"

—at the same instant Maxwell whispered to me. "That's him!"

Simultaneously the Kid must have seen, or felt, the presence of a third person at the head of the bed. He raised quickly his pistol, a self cocker, within a foot of my breast. Retreating rapidly across the room he cried: "Quien es? Quien es?" (*"Who's that? Who's that?"*)

All this occurred in a moment. Quickly as possible I drew my revolver and fired, threw my body aside, and fired again.

The second shot was useless; the Kid fell dead. He never spoke. A struggle or two, a little strangling sound as he gasped for breath, and the Kid was with his many victims.

Maxwell had plunged over the foot of the bed on the floor, dragging the bed-clothes with him. I went to the door and met Poe and McKinney there.

Maxwell rushed past me, out on the porch; they threw their guns down on him, when he cried: "Don't shoot, don't shoot."

I told my companions I had got the Kid. They asked me if I had not shot the wrong man. I told them I had made no blunder, that I knew the Kid's voice too well to be mistaken.

The Kid was entirely unknown to either of them. They had seen him pass in, and, as he stepped on the porch, McKinney, who was sitting, rose to his feet; one of his spurs caught under the boards, and nearly threw him.

The Kid laughed, but probably, saw their guns, as he drew his revolver and sprang into the doorway, as he hailed: "Who comes there?"

Seeing a bareheaded, barefooted man, in his shirt-sleeves, with a butcher knife in his hand, and hearing his hail in excellent Spanish, they naturally supposed him to be a Mexican and an attache of the establishment, hence their suspicion that I had shot the wrong man.

We now entered the room and examined the body. The ball struck him just above the heart, and must have cut through the ventricles.

Poe asked me how many shots I fired; I told him two, but that I had no idea where the second one went. Both Poe and McKinney said the Kid must have fired then, as there were surely three shots fired. I told them that he had fired one shot, between my two.

Maxwell said that the Kid fired; yet, when we came to look for bullet marks, none from his pistol could be found. We searched long and faithfully--found both my bullet marks and none other; so, against the impression and senses of four men, we had to conclude that the Kid did not fire at all.

We examined his pistol--a self-cocker, calibre 41. It had five cartridges and one shell in the chambers, the hammer resting on the shell, but this proves nothing, as many carry their revolvers in this way for safety; besides, this shell looked as though it had been shot some time before.

It will never be known whether the Kid recognized me or not. If he did, it was the first time, during all his life of peril, that he ever lost his presence of mind, or failed to shoot first and hesitate afterwards.

He knew that a meeting with me meant surrender or fight. He told several persons about Sumner that he bore no animosity against me, and had no desire to do me injury. He also said that he knew, should we meet, he would have to surrender, kill me, or get killed himself. So, he declared his intention, should we meet, to commence shooting on sight.

On the following morning, the alcalde, Alejandro Segura, held an inquest on the body.

Hon. M. Rudolph, of Sunnyside, was foreman of the coroner's jury. They found a verdict that William H. Bonney came to his death from a gun-shot wound, the weapon in the hands of Pat F. Garrett, that the fatal wound was inflicted by the said Garrett in the discharge of his official duty as sheriff, and that the homicide was justifiable.

The body was neatly and properly dressed and buried in the military cemetery at Fort Sumner, July 15, 1881.

DEAD OR ALIVE ?

His exact age, on the day of his death, was 21 years, 7 months, and 21 days.

Billy the Kid

From *The Authentic Life of Billy, the Kid*
by Pat Garrett.
Santa Fe: New Mexico Printing and Publishing Company,
1882

Have you enjoyed
reading these short stories?

~Please let others know!

- Write a review—even a brief one—on Amazon or other websites. Your recommendation creates interest among readers!

- Mention this book in your tweets, on Facebook, your blog, and in other social media.

- Share this copy with a friend—or give copies to all your friends. It's available as an ebook, as well as in this print edition.

Would you like to receive emails
(one a month, at most) **announcing new releases and special offers?**

Sign up on our website:

www.cleananpressBooks.com

You can also send your comments or questions to the author there.

Thank you for your interest and help.

Happy reading!

About the Author

Ellis Ash lives in Santa Fe, combs the beach on Pawleys Island, and writes in Paris.

Non-Fiction,
From the same publisher . . .

Billy the Kid's Jail
Santa Fe, New Mexico
by
Lynn Michelsohn

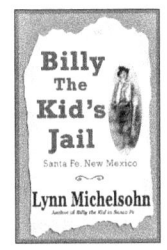

A Glimpse of History on the
Southwestern Frontier

(82 pages, paperback $7.95, ebook $2.99)

*Billy the Kid
in Santa Fe*
(A Non-Fiction Trilogy)
Book One: Young Billy
by
Lynn Michelsohn

Wild West history, Outlaw Legends, and
The City at the End of the Santa Fe Trail
(252 pages, paperback $17.95, ebook $9.99)